DANGEROUS
GHOSTS

DANGEROUS GHOSTS

DANIEL COHEN

G. P. PUTNAM'S SONS   NEW YORK

G. P. Putnam's Sons, a division of The Putnam & Grosset Group,
200 Madison Avenue, New York, NY 10016.
G. P. Putnam's Sons, Reg. U.S. Pat. & Tm. Off.
Published simultaneously in Canada
Printed in the United States of America
Book designed by Marikka Tamura
Text set in Baskerville

Library of Congress Cataloging-in-Publication Data

Cohen, Daniel, 1936–. Dangerous ghosts / Daniel Cohen   p.   cm.
Summary: A collection of seventeen tales about ghosts
drawn from a wide variety of sources from psychical research
to pure legend and folklore.
1. Ghosts—Juvenile literature. [1. Ghosts.] I. Title.
BF1461.C638   1995   95-45439 CIP AC   133.1—dc20
ISBN 0-399-22913-2

10 9 8 7 6 5 4 3 2 1

First Impression

In memory of Jeremy Brett.
He will be missed.

CONTENTS

INTRODUCTION   ". . . But I Am Afraid of Them"   1

CHAPTER 1   The Fate of the Dead   5

CHAPTER 2   Behind the Chair   8

CHAPTER 3   The Night Nurse's Story   12

CHAPTER 4   The High Priestess of Death   18

CHAPTER 5   Tregagle   23

CHAPTER 6   Hit by a Ghost, Bit by His Dog   27

CHAPTER 7   "He Is with Me Even Now"   31

CHAPTER 8   "The Meanest Ghost"   35

CHAPTER 9   The Terror of Glam   41

CHAPTER 10   The Choking Ghost   45

CHAPTER 11   Meeting on the Road   49

CHAPTER 12   The Bandaged Horror   53

CHAPTER 13   The Death Car Returns   57

CHAPTER 14   The Bloodstone Ring   62

CHAPTER 15   Waiting in the Shadows   71

CHAPTER 16   The Last Tenant   77

CHAPTER 17   Something in the Room   83

INTRODUCTION

"... BUT I AM AFRAID OF THEM"

THE MARQUISE DU DEFFAND, an eighteenth-century French woman of letters, was once asked, "Do you believe in ghosts?"

"Oh, no," she replied, "but I am afraid of them."

That is a very sensible point of view. Even those who don't *really* believe in ghosts, and I admit I am one of them, can still be frightened when entering a dark room or walking down a deserted road or hearing a strange noise.

In a sense I have "lived" with ghosts for many years now. I have heard the stories, read the accounts, visited haunted houses and graveyards, and attended séances and conferences about ghosts. In short, I have weighed the evidence. It's intriguing, sometimes puzzling, but all in all not enough to overwhelm the rational side of my mind, which keeps telling me there can't be any such thing.

And yet, I am afraid of them.

Writing is a solitary occupation. And more than once while sitting alone in my office at night, working on this book, I had to stop and go find human company because I had scared myself.

It's only a story, I said to myself, over and over. Even if someone believed this tale at one time, there is no good reason why a rational person living in the closing years of the twentieth century should be frightened. But if I really believed that right down to the core, why did I hesitate to turn around in a room that I knew was empty? Was it because I was afraid of seeing something that I knew couldn't or at least shouldn't be there?

There are all sorts of tales of friendly ghosts and benevolent spirits. There are people who say they feel comfortable in the presence of a ghost. For the rest of us, believers and nonbelievers alike, we are just plain scared.

What is it about ghosts that scares us so much?

I think it's mainly the feeling that a ghost is unnatural, alien to the world of the living. The unknown is always potentially dangerous.

Even someone who was kindly and well disposed toward us in life might, after death, be transformed into something evil. And of course, if the ghost had some reason to come back to trouble the living, revenge perhaps, then so much the worse.

Over the centuries and across many cultures, the lines between ghost, demon, and evil spirit have not been distinct. Sometimes there is no difference at all.

Then there is the widespread belief that mixing with ghosts, at any level and for any motive at all, is just not a good idea. Dealing with ghosts, which are not "of this world," involves "forbidden knowledge," and anyone who becomes involved with *that* is likely to suffer horribly.

The tales in this book have been drawn from a wide variety of sources, from psychical research, which tries to carefully investigate and document alleged ghostly events, to pure legend and folklore. My hope is that these stories will do to you what they did to me: create the feeling that something has just crept up behind you and made you too scared to turn around and see what it is.

CHAPTER ONE

THE FATE OF
THE DEAD

Sometimes it's better not to know!

FROM NORTHERN ITALY comes a tale of an old peasant couple who tried to know too much. One night they swore a solemn oath that whoever died first would try to return to tell the other what lay beyond the grave.

A few years later the man died. He was old. His heart had been failing for a long time, so his death was not unexpected.

The body was cleaned, dressed, and laid out properly in the couple's house. Friends and family came and went, paying their last respects and offering what comfort they could to the widow.

The old woman thanked the visitors but told them they

should go home. She preferred to spend the night before the burial alone with her husband's body.

She sat in a straight-backed chair next to the corpse and wondered where her husband's spirit was and if he would be able to return as he had solemnly pledged to do.

A sudden knock at the door caused the old woman to jump out of her chair. She half expected to see her husband's ghost standing outside. But at the door stood a tall young man carrying a long wooden staff. He was a stranger; she had never seen him before.

The stranger said that he was looking for shelter for the night. The old woman nodded toward the corpse laid out in the room, but the young man seemed neither alarmed nor surprised. He simply sat down on the other side of the corpse and gazed intently at it.

After about an hour an unearthly and terrible wailing sound was heard. It grew louder and was obviously coming from the corpse. Then the corpse began to sit up. Its face was contorted in agony.

Terrified, the old woman put her hands over her ears and rushed into the next room to hide from the horrible scene. The stranger rose and touched the forehead of the corpse with his stick. The eyes closed, and the corpse sank back onto the table.

Still shaking, the old woman came back into the room and sat down again. The stranger took his seat on the other side of the table that held the corpse.

For a while everything was quiet. Then in the distance,

church bells chimed. Even this familiar sound made the old woman begin to tremble in fear. But as the sound of the bells died away, the corpse once again began to move.

This time it did not rise slowly. It jumped off the table, its head jerking wildly from side to side. It suddenly rushed toward the old woman, grabbed her by the throat, and began to choke her.

The corpse cried out in a hollow voice that sounded as if it came from far away, "I am in hell! You put me there! I'll make you pay!"

The stranger ran across the room and again touched his wooden staff to the corpse's forehead. It relaxed its grip on the woman's throat.

From the point where the stranger's staff had touched the dead man's forehead, the body began to melt like a wax candle. Finally only a broken skeleton and a bundle of clothes lay upon the floor.

Now the old woman fell to the floor beside the remains. She began to cry and wail and beg for forgiveness and mercy. The stranger helped her to her feet and walked her over to her chair.

"It is not for the living to know the fate of the dead," he said. Then he opened the door and walked off into the darkness.

CHAPTER TWO

BEHIND THE CHAIR

IN 1941 BRITAIN WAS AT WAR. A group of young officers was taken to dinner by an older man who had served as an officer in World War I.

During the dinner conversation, one of the young men said that he and the others in his group had recently been staying in a large country house in the county of Dorset. During both World War I and World War II, it was common practice for soldiers to be housed temporarily in large private homes.

The young man's host was extremely interested. He knew the house in question very well. "It's a really beautiful place. That must have been extremely pleasant."

The young officer seemed embarrassed. "Well, sir, it wasn't, actually."

"Oh? Why?"

"Well, sir, you'll probably laugh at me. We didn't like it be-cause it was haunted."

The host assured the young man that he would not laugh and was most anxious about what had happened.

"I suppose it wasn't much, really," the young officer said, "but somehow we all got an overpowering, almost crushing sense of evil. The owner of the mansion had to leave on forty-eight hours' notice, and before we moved in, he had removed or stored most of the art treasures—all except one picture of a woman over the mantelpiece in the dining room. This paint-ing, the owner had told our colonel, must be left exactly where it was and on no account be moved. Well, we had put a dart-board up beside it, and one evening during play the frame was chipped by a dart. The colonel was very angry. He said that a dart would pierce the woman next, and as the picture was almost certainly valuable, he was going to take it down and store it. He did, and it was after that that the trouble started."

"Do, please, go on."

"It doesn't sound like very much. We used to lie in bed with the curtains drawn back, looking at the stars. On moonlit nights the moon would shine into the bedroom and reflect off the polished door handle. We used to watch the door handle turning, and the door would open. We couldn't see anything, but there was a filthy sense of evil, and sometimes we almost felt we were being followed around. I'm afraid that's all, sir."

The other young officers at the table, who all had been at the house in Dorset, agreed that the events were reported ac-curately.

"I think," remarked their host quietly, "that I may be able to throw a little light on this. By an odd coincidence, during the first war, in 1917, I had been wounded and was sent to recuperate in Dorset. I stayed with an elderly lady in that exact neighborhood. This lady knew all the local history and told me what many people believed, that the mansion you stayed in had once been the scene of tragedy."

He continued, "Isn't it strange how history repeats itself? In 1806, or thereabouts, a regiment was quartered nearby against the threat of an invasion from France. The general was asked to dine at your house, and his host asked him to bring along one of his young staff members. There was going to be quite a big party, with dancing afterward.

"While dinner was in progress, the general saw, much to his amazement, that the young officer, whom he knew well, was behaving in a most unusual and rude way. Although he was seated between two very attractive young women, he took absolutely no notice of them. Instead he was staring with a look of absolute horror at his hostess, who sat beside the general at the head table. The general was getting angry, and he tried by coughing and frowning to get the officer's attention and bring him back to his senses.

"It didn't have any effect. Suddenly the young man jumped up from the table and shouted, 'I can't bear it.' He pushed back his chair and rushed out of the room. The general followed immediately, thinking that the young man had gone mad. In the courtyard the general found that his officer had just ridden away. He mounted his own horse and followed.

The general had a faster horse and was able to overtake him. He caught hold of the runaway's horse's bridle. 'Have you lost your senses?' he shouted. 'What is going on?'

" 'Maybe I have,' gasped the young man. 'No one else seemed to see it. But I saw a hooded figure standing close behind the woman next to you, and it was *willing* her to commit suicide!'

" 'Nonsense, nonsense, my boy!' said the general, who really did believe that his officer had gone crazy.

"At that moment the hoofbeats of a third horse were heard. The rider, who was approaching at a breakneck speed, was one of the servants from the house.

" 'Where in God's name are you going?' cried the general.

" 'To fetch the doctor,' the man answered. 'But I fear it is too late. Just after you both left, Madam picked up a table knife and cut her throat in front of everyone.'

"I believe that the picture you saw at the house was a portrait of the dead woman."

CHAPTER THREE

THE NIGHT NURSE'S STORY

IN THE DAYS BEFORE the condition of a critically ill patient was monitored by a variety of electronic devices, it was common to have a patient watched by a nurse twenty-four hours a day. Usually the nurses worked in shifts, a day nurse and a night nurse. Nurse Mackenzie was such a nurse.

Shortly after she had received her training at a hospital in Edinburgh, Scotland, she was sent to a hotel called the White Dove in Edinburgh. One of the guests at the hotel, a woman named Vinning, had become very sick.

The owner of the hotel knew nothing about the sick woman except her name and the fact that at one time she had been an actress. He noticed that she had looked ill on her arrival the previous week. Two days after her arrival, she complained of feeling as though she had a high fever. A doctor was sent for, and he diagnosed Miss Vinning as suffering from a serious disease that was rare in England, though fairly common in warmer countries like India.

The woman soon lapsed into unconsciousness, and two nurses were sent for by the doctor to watch the patient day and night. Nurse Mackenzie's hours were from 9 P.M. until 9 A.M.

The hotel was an old one, but it had been newly renovated and equipped with all the conveniences available at the time, like electric lights. The room in which the sick woman lay was rather cheerfully decorated, but it somehow filled Nurse Mackenzie with a feeling of depression and dread. She felt that there was something "hideous and repulsive" in the room.

It was not the patient, Miss Vinning, who, despite her illness, was a very good-looking woman. She was also far too ill and too heavily drugged to say anything. She groaned and turned once in a while, but that was about all.

The first night Nurse Mackenzie spent at Miss Vinning's bedside was uneventful. The patient even showed some signs of improvement. The second night was different. A storm had broken outside. The wind was raging, and rain was pelting the window of the room.

Nurse Mackenzie had been on the job for about two hours when she looked up from the book she was reading and saw, sitting in a chair beside the head of the bed, a child, "a tiny girl." Nurse Mackenzie could not imagine how she had gotten there. "I could only suppose that the shrieking of the wind down the wide chimney had deadened the sound of the door and her footsteps."

Nurse Mackenzie was angry that the child had not knocked before entering the sickroom. She got up from her chair and was about to order the girl out of the room, when the girl lifted a hand and motioned her back. "I obeyed because I could not help myself," said the nurse.

The child was dressed in a rather peculiar fashion. She had a wide-brimmed hat, which completely obscured her features. To the Scottish nurse there was something about the style of the dress "that suggested foreign nationality, [possibly] the Orient."

Nurse Mackenzie heard her patient sigh, and she looked over toward the sick woman. "She was tossing to and fro on the blankets and breathing in the most agonized manner, as if in delirium or caught in a particularly dreadful nightmare." The nurse was alarmed by this, and she tried frantically to overcome the spell that she seemed to be under—but without success. She sank back into her chair and closed her eyes. When she opened them again, the child was gone.

"A tremendous feeling of relief surged through me and, jumping out of my seat, I hastened to the bedside—my patient was worse, the fever had increased and she was delirious."

After a few hours, however, the sick woman seemed to improve and drifted into a peaceful sleep. By morning she gave every appearance of having recovered from her relapse.

When Nurse Mackenzie told the doctor about the child's visit, he became very angry.

"Whatever happens, Nurse," the doctor said, "take care that no one enters the room tonight; the patient's condition is far too critical for her to see anyone, even her own daughter. You must keep the door locked."

Armed with those orders, Nurse Mackenzie carefully locked the door the following evening after she went on duty. She sat down by the fire. The storm had ended, but there had been a heavy fall of snow and the weather had turned bitterly cold.

The sick woman was sleeping peacefully, and Nurse Mackenzie herself dozed off. At about quarter to one in the morning, the nurse was awakened by what sounded like a sob coming from the bed. She looked up, and there, seated in the same place as the previous evening, was the child with the wide-brimmed hat. The nurse sprang out of her chair, but again the child raised her hand. "As before, I collapsed—spellbound, paralyzed."

Nurse Mackenzie sat in horror, listening to the moans coming from the sick woman. "Every second she grew worse, and each sound rang in my ears like the hammering of nails in her coffin."

Then the sounds stopped. The child got up from the chair and walked toward the window, and the spell was broken. Said Nurse Mackenzie, "With a cry of indignation I literally bounded over the carpet and faced the intruder."

"Who are you?" the nurse hissed. "Tell me your name instantly! How dare you enter this room without my permission!"

It is probably not wise to challenge an apparition under any circumstances. It certainly wasn't wise in this case. The child raised her head, and the nurse snatched away the hat. She found herself looking not at the face of a living child but staring into the face of a corpse. It was the corpse of a child that Nurse Mackenzie thought to be Indian. "In its lifetime the child had, without doubt, been lovely; it was now horrible—horrible with all the ghastly disfigurements . . . of a long consignment to the grave." Worst of all was a gaping cut in the throat.

This terrifying sight caused the nurse to faint. When she regained consciousness, she found that the ghost was gone and that her patient was dead. One of the dead woman's arms was thrown across her eyes, as if she wanted to shut out something that she was afraid to look at.

It was part of the nurse's duties to help pack up the belongings of the dead woman. One of the things she found was a large envelope that had a postmark from a city in India. The nurse was trying to find some clue to where the dead woman's relatives might be contacted. She opened the envelope. It contained only a large photograph of a pretty young Indian girl. "I recognized the dress immediately—it was that of my ghostly visitor." On the back of the photograph were written the words "Natalie. May God forgive us both."

No other information about Miss Vinning or the unknown

Natalie was ever discovered. After a time the inquiry was abandoned. The ghost of the Indian child was never seen again at the hotel. But the hotel is still haunted—haunted by the ghost of a woman.

CHAPTER FOUR

THE HIGH PRIESTESS
OF DEATH

PRACTICALLY EVERYONE has heard of King Tut's Curse. It is
the curse that is supposedly attached to the tomb of the
pharaoh Tutankhamen. Tutankhamen's tomb, the only un-
plundered tomb of an ancient Egyptian king ever found, was
discovered in 1922. A short time after the discovery, Lord
Carnarvon, who had financed the expedition, died in Cairo
under mysterious circumstances. Over the years the story of
the curse has grown as others connected with the discovery
also met strange or unexplained deaths.

But there is another, earlier story of an ancient Egyptian
curse that may have been far more effective.

In the late nineteenth century there were a large number
of archaeological discoveries in Egypt. Often the finds were

made by people who were little better than tomb robbers. The artifacts, including mummy cases and the mummies themselves, regularly wound up in the markets of Cairo or other Egyptian cities. There they were offered for sale to wealthy collectors, and among the most eager collectors of these "curiosities," as the artifacts were often called at the time, were Englishmen.

One such collector was a man named Douglas Murray. In a shop in the backstreets of Cairo he was shown a mummy case. It was supposed to have belonged to a high priestess in the Temple of Amon Ra, chief god of the ancient Egyptians. The priestess was said to have lived in the city of Thebes in about 1600 B.C.

As with most mummy cases, this one bore a likeness of the person whose mummy was inside. The likeness on this case was particularly well preserved. Usually these mummy case drawings—and thousands of them have been found—are stiff and formal. They have no individuality, and it is hard to tell one from another. But there was something unsettling about this particular likeness. One man who viewed it declared that "the expression on the face was that of a soul in living torment." It certainly was different.

When Murray first saw the object, he was quite repelled by it. But it was an unusually fine example of ancient Egyptian art, and quite a bargain to boot. So he bought it and had it packed up for shipment to London along with other curiosities he had purchased during his Egyptian travels.

Then the misfortunes began. A few days after he bought

the mummy case, Murray went on a shooting expedition up the Nile. The gun that he was carrying exploded in his hand, for no known reason. His hand and arm were seriously injured, and he was in agony. The boat was quickly turned around to return to Cairo so Murray could get urgent medical attention. But the boat encountered strong head winds— very unusual at that time of year—and the return journey took ten days. By the time Murray reached Cairo, gangrene had set in. He lay in the hospital for weeks, feverish and near death. He did recover, but the infected arm had to be amputated above the elbow.

Some of Murray's companions suffered even worse fates. Two of them died on the return voyage to England and were buried at sea. Two servants who had handled the mummy case died within a year.

When the ship carrying Murray and the curiosities finally docked in London, it was found that the valuable objects all had been stolen. Perhaps they had never even left Cairo. Murray had been too ill to keep careful track of his possessions.

No—not everything had been stolen. The high priestess's mummy case was still there. For some reason the thieves had rejected it. Murray gazed at the portrait and felt that the eyes seemed to come to life and glare at him with a malevolence that turned his blood cold. He sensed that all the terrible things that had happened to him were somehow connected to that mummy case.

Murray decided to give the case away to a lady he knew.

As soon as she received the strange gift, the lady suffered a string of disasters. Her mother sustained what should have been a trivial leg injury. But the leg failed to heal as it should, and the poor woman died after months of prolonged suffering. The lady's fiancé decided abruptly, and for no particular reason, that he no longer wanted to marry her. Her pets died. Then the lady herself became ill. The doctors were at a loss to diagnose the nature of her illness, but she became so weak that she was afraid she too would die. She called her lawyer to make out her will.

The lawyer made out the will, but on hearing the whole story, he also suggested that the mummy case be returned to Douglas Murray. As soon as she did that, her health recovered. However, Murray's health was broken, and he certainly didn't want the mummy case back. So he donated it to the British Museum. Surely this large and impersonal institution could not be affected by long-dead Egyptian priestesses.

Or could it? A photographer who took a series of photographs of the mummy case for the museum died mysteriously a few weeks later. An Egyptologist who was in charge of the object while the museum decided whether or not to accept it died suddenly and unexpectedly.

But finally the museum did accept the mummy case. It was put on display in 1889 as Exhibit No. 22542 in the second Egyptian Room of the British Museum.

The reputation of the high priestess's mummy case was by that time well known. Stories about its evil influence had appeared in the press. Visitors to the museum laid bunches of flowers on the floor in front of the exhibit to appease the spirit of the long-dead Theban priestess. People would gather around the exhibit to gape and whisper. It became a magnet for occultists and all who believed in the supernatural.

Finally the museum just got tired of answering an endless stream of questions about the mummy case. It was removed from public view and stored in the basement with countless other objects in the museum's vast collection.

The sudden disappearance of this notorious exhibit prompted what was surely the most dramatic story of all. It was said that the museum had secretly sold the mummy case to an American collector, and that it had been shipped to America in the cargo hold of the *Titanic*. In 1912 the *Titanic*, the largest and most luxurious ocean liner ever built, a ship that was supposed to be unsinkable, struck an iceberg in the North Atlantic on her maiden voyage from England to America and sank, with a terrible loss of life.

No one knows exactly where or how this particular rumor began. Spokesmen for the British Museum insist that the mummy case had never been sold to an American and that it was not aboard the *Titanic*, but they didn't put it back on display either, and the rumors have never really died out.

So the high priestess's mummy case remains in the basement of the British Museum—or at the bottom of the North Atlantic.

CHAPTER FIVE

TREGAGLE

IN THE DISTRICT of England called Cornwall, the howling wind that comes before a storm is often called a Tregagle. A crying child can also be called a Tregagle. Anybody who talks loudly may be told that he is "worse than Tregagle."

These all are references to a very popular story about the ghost of a man called Jan Tregagle.

The story is old, and the versions differ. According to one account, Tregagle was in life the "Cornwall Bluebeard"—a notorious wife killer. But more numerous versions speak of him as something less sinister—a crooked lawyer and magistrate who lived in the town of Trevorder during the seventeenth century.

The traditions say that Tregagle was born poor but became

rich and powerful by taking bribes to lose his poorer clients' cases, finding false witnesses, and forging legal documents. It was also whispered that he had murdered his own wife and sister, but such rumors are inevitably attached to those who have bad reputations.

Why anyone would trust a lawyer with such a reputation is hard to imagine. But one man apparently did trust him. This man lent a large sum of money to a neighbor. He never received any written acknowledgment of the loan. The only evidence he had was provided by Tregagle, who served as a witness to the transaction.

But Tregagle died soon afterward. When the lender asked for his money, the borrower said simply that he had never received any.

The whole matter wound up in court. The lender swore that Tregagle had witnessed the loan. Under oath, the borrower denied this and said, "If Tregagle ever saw it, I wish to God that Tregagle may come and declare it."

That was an unwise statement. Tregagle was just about the last man anyone would wish to call back from the grave. Ghosts sometimes have a way of appearing when they are summoned, and that is what happened. The door to the court swung open to reveal the rotting form of the dead Jan Tregagle. He pointed to the debtor and said, "I can no more be a false witness. Thou hast the money and found it easy to bring me from the grave, but thou wilt not find it so easy to put me away."

When the borrower left the court, the ghost of Tregagle followed him. Wherever the man went, there was Tregagle's spirit. It was by his side night and day. It never let him rest. The badly frightened man begged the judges of the court somehow to get rid of the ghost. But the judges were not at all sympathetic.

"That is thy business," they said. "Thou has brought him, thou mayest get rid of him."

In desperation the borrower paid back the money he owed. But the ghost of Tregagle still would not depart. The man gave money to the poor in the hopes that good deeds would cause the ghost to disappear. It didn't work. Finally the haunted man called on a variety of people, from ministers to magicians, who were supposed to be experienced at "laying a ghost," sending it back to where it came from.

These wise men were able to "bind" the ghost—that is, get control of it. They took Tregagle's spirit to a place called Dosmery Pool, which was reputed to be bottomless. There the spirit was supposed to empty the pool using only a small seashell with a hole in it.

The pool, however, was not bottomless, and Tregagle managed the task in a short time. He then immediately returned to torment worse than ever the man who had called him from the grave.

So the exorcists were called for once again. This time they took the haunted man to an open field and drew a circle around him. Tregagle's spirit then assumed the form of a black bull and tried to get at him. The spirit bellowed and roared and could be heard for miles around.

But slowly the spirit of Tregagle calmed down and was led away. This time he was taken to a place called Gwenvor Cove. There he was given the task of making a bundle of sand, tying it up with a rope of sand, and carrying it miles away to a place called Carn Olva, a high granite cliff.

An impossible task—or so those who bound the spirit thought. But then there was a very cold winter. The ghost of Jan Tregagle took water from a nearby brook, poured it over the sand, where it froze solid, and carried the bundle in triumph to Carn Olva.

The spirit then immediately flew back to the man who had raised him in the first place, and probably would have torn the poor fellow to pieces if the spirit layers had not intervened once again. This time they took Tregagle to the shore of the ocean and gave him the same task. But now he was not allowed to go near fresh water—and on the Cornish coast the ocean water does not freeze. It is said that he is there still and can be heard roaring before a storm comes in.

Tregagle is a popular spirit in Cornwall, and the stories have become more confusing than ever. Guidebooks, which often list the local ghosts among an area's attractions, have Tregagle appearing in half a dozen different locations.

CHAPTER SIX

HIT BY A GHOST, BIT BY HIS DOG

THE SOCIETY FOR PSYCHICAL RESEARCH (SPR) was established in England more than a century ago. It was the SPR's aim to investigate strange events and phenomena that seemed to lie outside the boundaries of orthodox science. One of the things the SPR did was to collect what we might call ghost stories.

The SPR didn't want legends or folklore or tales of hauntings that occurred long ago. The organization was looking for firsthand accounts of encounters with ghosts that could somehow be checked and verified. They collected thousands of such accounts. But the story told by Mr. James Durham was a highly unusual one. In most SPR cases, the ghost was seen or heard, but rarely felt in such a direct and physical fashion.

At the end of the nineteenth century, James Durham was

a watchman at the railroad station in the town of Darlington. He had been employed there for several years and had the reputation of being a regular and conscientious worker. Everyone who knew him insisted that he was an extremely honest man, not given to telling lies or playing practical jokes. When James Durham said something, people believed him.

In a letter written to the SPR, Durham said, "I used to go on duty about 8 P.M. and come off at 6 A.M. . . . One night during winter and about midnight or 12:30, I was feeling rather cold with standing here and there; I said to myself, 'I will away down and get something to eat.' There was a porter's cellar where a fire was kept on . . ."

Durham went down into the porter's cellar, took off his coat, sat down on the bench in front of the small gas fire, and turned up the gas. As soon as he did this, a strange man entered the cellar from an adjoining room. The man was followed by a big black dog, probably a retriever.

"As soon as he entered, my eye was upon him and his eye upon me, and we were intently watching each other as he moved on to the front of the fire. There he stood looking at me, and a curious smile came over his countenance. He had a stand-up collar and a cut-away coat with gilt buttons and a Scotch cap. All at once he struck at me, and I had the impression that he hit me. I up with my fist and struck back at him. My fist seemed to go through him and struck against the stone above the fireplace, and knocked the skin off my knuckles. The man seemed to be struck back into the fire and uttered a strange unearthly squeak. Immediately the dog gripped me by the calf of my leg, and seemed to cause me pain.

"The man recovered his position, called off the dog with a sort of click of the tongue, then went back into [the adjoining room], followed by the dog. I lighted my lantern, and looked into the room, but there was neither dog nor man, and no outlet for them except the one by which they had entered."

Durham concluded, quite reasonably, "I was satisfied that what I had seen was ghostly."

Durham repeated the story of his experience to his fellow workmen. And it caused quite a commotion. A lot of people asked him about it. A man Durham called Old Edward Pease, "father of railways," sent for him. "He and others put this question to me, 'Are you sure you were not asleep and had the nightmare?' My answer was quite sure, for I had not been a minute in the cellar and was just going to get something to eat. I was certainly not under the influence of strong drink, I have always been a non-drinker. My mind at the time was perfectly free from trouble."

That wasn't all. What really got people excited was that many years before, a clerk named Winter, who had worked in the station at Darlington, shot himself, and his body had been carried down to the very spot where Durham had seen the ghost. Durham had never known Winter and had not heard that anyone had ever committed suicide at the station. Yet, "Mr. Pease, and others who had known him, told me my description exactly corresponded to his appearance and the way he dressed and also that he had a black retriever just like the one which gripped me. I should add that no mark or effect remained on the spot where I seemed to be seized."

Nor was there any mark where the ghost had apparently struck out at Durham. However, there is no doubt that the watchman had badly skinned his knuckles trying to hit the ghost, going right through the form and hitting the wall.

Investigators for the SPR visited the scene of what they called "the battle with the ghost" and found it exactly as Durham had described it. One of them wrote, "It is the only instance which I remember in which an apparition attempted to injure, and even in this solitary instance there was no real harm done."

CHAPTER SEVEN

"HE IS WITH ME EVEN NOW"

ABOARD SHIP DURING the eighteenth century, the captain's word was law. There were no higher authorities. So long as a ship remained at sea, there was no one to whom an ordinary seaman could appeal, no matter how mistreated he was.

There were good captains, bad captains, and everything in between. On this particular ship, the captain was one of the bad ones. He was a heavy drinker with a quick temper and an utter disdain for his crew. Not surprisingly the crew was sullen and uncooperative without being openly rebellious.

The captain knew how his crew felt—but he could not operate a ship without a crew. So he focused all his anger on a man called Bill Jones. Jones was probably the oldest man aboard—too old and too fat really to perform his tasks properly. The captain was sure that Jones was deliberately moving slowly just to annoy him. He constantly screamed and cursed at the man. But Jones was not intimidated. He just continued to do his own work at his own pace.

But one day during a particularly vicious harangue, something in the old seaman snapped. He turned on the captain and lashed back with a string of oaths that stunned the captain and astounded the rest of the crew. Bill Jones shouted out what they all had been thinking but had been afraid to say.

The captain could almost feel the contempt that everyone on board had for him. He couldn't stand it. Trembling with rage, he rushed down the corridor to his cabin. The captain came back carrying a blunderbuss, an old-fashioned type of rifle, that was packed with nails and pieces of iron. He found Bill Jones standing where he had left him, and fired the gun point-blank at him.

The blast tore a terrible hole in the old sailor's chest. He was dying, but he had enough strength left to look directly at the captain and say, in a surprisingly firm voice, "Sir, you have done me now, but I will never leave you." He died almost immediately after uttering those words.

While a captain had almost unlimited authority aboard his ship, he did not possess the authority to kill a sailor simply because he disliked him. The captain knew that when the ship returned to England, questions would be asked about the fate of the missing seaman. He made his crew swear that they would say Jones had become ill, died, and was buried at sea. Whether they would keep their oath once they returned home and were beyond the captain's power, he could not be sure.

But the captain had more immediate problems. True to his dying words, Bill Jones had not left. The ghost of the murdered seaman was not generally visible to the ordinary sailors. But they were able to detect its presence by a row of casks that seemed to have shifted by themselves, or by a brass fitting that was being polished by a rag guided by an unseen hand. The elderly sailor, it seemed, was still performing his old tasks in his same old slow way. Every once in a while a sailor would apparently catch a glimpse of Jones's bulky figure, but as soon as the observer became aware of the figure, it was gone.

The captain, however, saw the ghost constantly. He confided to his first mate that it always seemed to be hovering around him. If he awoke in the middle of the night, it was at the foot of the bed, staring at him. He was so distraught that he could no longer exercise command of the ship and asked the mate to take over for him.

The crew watched with a sort of horrified fascination as the captain seemed literally to waste away from day to day. He barely ate anything. He didn't ever seem to sleep. He would just pace back and forth across the deck, and every few seconds he would turn his head to the side, as if to look at what no one else could see.

One day the captain apparently could stand it no longer. The mate heard a splash, as if something had been thrown overboard. He looked over the railing and saw the captain in the water. He was not struggling, trying to save himself. On the contrary, he looked like a man intent upon drowning.

But quite suddenly the doomed man began to thrash about wildly. And the mate heard him shout out, "He is with me even now!" just before he disappeared beneath the waves for the last time.

CHAPTER EIGHT

"THE MEANEST GHOST"

DANTON WALKER was a popular New York columnist during the 1940s and 1950s. He was also a man with a deep and serious interest in the subject of ghosts.

Walker would often entertain his readers with ghostly tales that he had heard from his celebrity friends. Most of the ghosts Walker wrote about were benign; some were downright friendly. But there were a few who did not have such sunny dispositions. This is one that he regarded as "the meanest ghost that ever lived . . ." a contradiction in terms, perhaps, but the meaning is clear enough.

Walker heard the story from Jeanne Owen, who was president of the New York chapter of the Wine and Food Society. Mrs. Owen's son George was interested in agriculture, and he bought an old farm, called Spring Hill Farm, in the Napa valley of California. At the time it was quite an isolated place, reached only by four miles of bumpy dirt road from the little town of St. Helena.

The farm was in a rundown condition when George Owen bought it. The buildings were in particularly bad shape, because no one had lived in them for years. George had the old farmhouse remodeled into a comfortable modern house for himself, his wife, Dorothy, and their new baby.

The driveway was covered over with gravel to keep it from turning into a sea of mud during the winter rains. A gravel driveway serves another purpose, as anyone who has ever had one knows. The crunching of the gravel signals the approach of a car or even a pedestrian.

In back of the main farmhouse and a short way up the hill was another building—a shack, everybody called it. It was a dismal little two-room cabin that seemed too small to be a place for people to live and too large to be a chicken house. George had no idea what it had been used for, and when he started making improvements on the property, he just left the shack alone. There were more immediate and pressing projects to take care of.

Jeanne Owen made a couple of trips to visit her son and his family. Though she liked the Napa valley and found the remodeled farmhouse quite comfortable, she also found staying there a troubling experience.

She slept in the guest room in the front of the house. And every night between the hours of midnight and about 2 A.M., she was awakened by the sound of footsteps going up and down the gravel drive. She wondered who in the world could be walking on the drive at that hour of the night. She went to the window and looked. But even on nights when the area was brilliantly illuminated by moonlight, she saw nothing. Until one night . . .

George Owen and his wife had a dog, a big German shepherd named Nick, that was part pet, part watchdog.

"Nick was an excellent and protective watchdog," Jeanne said, "and I felt sure he would never permit anything *living* to approach the house. The sound of the footsteps on the gravel always awakened him too. He would start growling; then he would jump off the porch and start in pursuit of some invisible object, only to return, whimpering as if he had been struck!"

On one very bright moonlit night, Jeanne did think she saw "something." It looked like the shadow of a man. "It moved to the end of the gravel drive and disappeared around the corner of the house, beyond which was a narrow path that led to the shack on the hill!"

The dog also saw the shadow and tried to chase it. But after a few seconds he came back whimpering, apparently in pain.

Jeanne tried to talk to her son and his wife about the experiences, but they refused to take her seriously.

If Jeanne Owen had been the only person to have heard the steps on the gravel drive, she might have dismissed them as a product of her own overactive imagination. Then one day she met a doctor friend of her daughter-in-law. He had been an overnight visitor at the farm on several occasions. During the course of the conversation, he said, "I would give anything to know who it is that walks on the gravel drive in front of the house every night between twelve and two, then disappears to nowhere. It bothered the dog too."

Still, after Jeanne returned to New York and some time passed, the whole incident faded from her mind, until she received a very disturbing letter from her daughter-in-law, Dorothy.

Dorothy described how she and George had been having dinner one evening when they saw the figure of a tall, gaunt old man smoking a cigarette walk out of the back hall and toward the front door. They didn't know who he was or how he had gotten into the house, but they knew he shouldn't be there. Their first concern was for the baby. They rushed to the bedroom and were deeply relieved to find him sleeping peacefully. There was no other sign of the gaunt old man except the lingering smell of stale cigarette smoke.

This completely unnerving experience prompted Dorothy to take her mother-in-law's story more seriously and to try to find out more about the history of the farm. She visited a neighbor, an eighty-five-year-old woman who knew the history of every family and every farm for miles around. She knew the history of Spring Hill Farm very well.

Originally the only house on the property was the two-room shack. It was occupied by a farmer and his wife. She was a good, hard-working farm woman. He was a strange, secretive, and miserly man. They had three sons, and somehow they continued to live in the tiny, cramped cabin without electricity, running water, or conveniences of any kind.

As the boys were growing up, they promised their mother that one day they were going to build her a "real" house. And when they were old enough they did just that. They built the farmhouse with their own hands on a lower slope. The construction went on despite their father's violent objections. And when it was finished, he flew into a furious rage and swore that they would never live in the new house, that he would kill them and burn the house down before he would let them move out of the cabin. They took the threat seriously, and one day the boys and their mother just left. They abandoned the farm and the house they had never lived in. But most important they abandoned the tyrannical and dangerous old man.

The old man continued to live in the shack. He became stranger and more isolated than ever. People saw less and less of him, until one day they realized that he had not been visible for several weeks. A group of men went up to the shack and found him dead inside his locked cabin. No one even bothered to find out what he had died from. They just buried him in an unmarked grave.

After that, Spring Hill Farm got a reputation for being haunted. No one claimed it, and no one wanted to live in it, until George Owen bought the farm and he and his family moved in. It is possible that the sight of a happy family living in that house made the angry old man's spirit angrier than ever.

That wasn't the end of the story. A few weeks after Dorothy learned the history of the farm, George had to go to San Francisco on business for a couple of days. On the first night, Dorothy was awakened by the barking of her dog and the smell of smoke. She got up to investigate and found that the back porch and the kitchen were in flames. She grabbed the baby, rushed into the living room to call the fire department in nearby St. Helena, and then fled from the house.

The fire department soon arrived; in fact the whole town pitched in to fight the blaze. But it was too late. The flames spread rapidly, and soon there was nothing left but a charred ruin. The cause of the fire was undetermined but suspicious, particularly since it had spread so quickly.

George Owen was not about to leave Spring Hill Farm. When he rebuilt his house, he moved it from the original site. He figured that the ghost of the old man hated the house that his sons had built for their mother, and he wasn't going to take any more chances.

After the new house was built, they never had any trouble—no mysterious footsteps, no shadows, no gaunt old man lurking around. The ghost was apparently satisfied. In any event, it was gone.

CHAPTER NINE

THE TERROR OF GLAM

MOST OF THE GHOSTS that we are familiar with, no matter how evilly inclined they might be, are not physical. That is, they might scare a person to death, but it is unlikely that they will beat him to death.

But in northern Europe, ghostly beliefs are very different. There, belief is strong in creatures called "walkers after death." They are more like moving corpses than the semi-transparent and ethereal beings we commonly think of as ghosts. These walkers are always enemies of the living, and they are most dangerous during the long and bitterly cold northern winter nights.

Of the many stories told about these ghostly creatures, the tale of Glam, which comes from Iceland, is the most famous.

Glam was a shepherd. He was an ugly and surly fellow with

a violent temper and no friends. He worked for a farmer named Thorhall, tending the farmer's flocks in isolated pastures. The solitary existence suited Glam.

One winter night Glam was at the farmhouse. He got into an argument with Thorhall over something. It was so trivial that no one could even remember how the argument had started or what it was really about. But in a blind fury, Glam stalked out of the house and into the snowstorm that was raging outside. He did not come back.

The next morning after the storm had let up, local farmers found Glam's mutilated corpse. It was surrounded by bloody footprints. Everyone assumed that he had met a walker. The farmers heaped a pile of stones over the body— a traditional form of burial in a place where the land was usually too solidly frozen to be dug up—and gratefully went home. They didn't want to be out after dark.

It was no good. Glam would not stay buried beneath the stones. That very night something attacked Thorhall's farm and killed all his horses. Night after night the family huddled inside their house while the thing prowled around, howling and banging on the door and walls. Occasionally the farmer would catch a glimpse of a hulking, shambling figure. Thorhall thought he recognized the form of the shepherd Glam. Either the dead man's body had been possessed by the spirit of a walker, or Glam had become a walker himself. It made little difference. No one could venture out of the farmhouse during the long hours of darkness. All of the animals in the outbuildings were killed. Finally Thorhall and his family had to abandon the farm entirely.

When summer arrived and the days were long, Thorhall was able to reclaim his farm, because Glam had no power in the daylight. But as the year progressed and the days grew shorter, Glam's power increased, and by autumn the ghost's rampages were as deadly as before.

Naturally word of the terrible haunting spread. Finally the stories came to the attention of Grettir, a man of great strength and size. He was known as Grettir the Strong. He decided to challenge the ghost.

One winter night Grettir came to the farmhouse. He wrapped himself in a furred cloak to keep out the cold and to conceal himself from whatever might come. And then he waited.

For hours nothing happened. Then something that was vaguely human in shape, smelling like rotted flesh, stumbled and lumbered into the room. It seemed to know instinctively that a man was concealed in the cloak. It pulled at the cloak, and Grettir jumped up to confront the monster.

The mortal and the ghost circled each other. Grettir, who was renowned for his wrestling skills, was confident that he could overcome even this thing from beyond the grave. He didn't bother to draw his dagger. But he had underestimated Glam's strength. They struggled back and forth. Glam continually tried to drag the man toward the door. The ghost's strength was renewed by the cold and the darkness. For his part, Grettir tried to keep the battle in the house, within the walls of the living.

Slowly Glam managed to move the fight closer and closer to the door. Grettir was about to be pulled outside, into the ghost's world. He braced himself against the doorframe. Then suddenly he released his grip and lunged toward Glam. This move caught the ghost off balance, and he fell backward on the ground. The creature was unable to rise. But it was able to speak in a harsh and clicking voice.

The ghost predicted that Grettir would become isolated and friendless and would forever see the world through the eyes of Glam.

Horrified, Grettir took out his dagger and cut the monster's throat to silence its voice. He then took the body and burned it. Whatever remained from the fire he buried in an isolated place.

Glam never bothered the farm of Thorhall again. But the ghost's prediction came true. During the fight, Grettir must have absorbed some of the spirit of Glam. He became increasingly evil-tempered and sullen. He began to hate the company of others, yet he was afraid to be alone. In the dark he began to see phantoms that were always hovering about, grabbing at him. People began to say that he saw with a "ghost's sight."

The great hero became a frightened recluse, feared and despised by others. When he died a few years later, there was no one to mourn for him.

In the end it was Glam who had really prevailed.

CHAPTER TEN

THE CHOKING GHOST

DURING THE FIRST HALF of the twentieth century, Elliott O'Donnell was one of the most prominent investigators of ghosts and collectors of ghost stories in the world. He always described himself as a rational man confronting the supernatural and the occult. And he swore that the stories he told were true, or at least had been reported to him as true, and he had good reason to believe his informants.

Before O'Donnell became involved with ghosts, he had a brief career in the theater, and he made many friends in the acting profession. One day while visiting Glasgow, Scotland, O'Donnell ran across an old theatrical acquaintance named Hely Browne. And Browne had a remarkable tale to tell him.

Hely Browne was part of a touring company that played Glasgow. When he arrived in the city, he found that all of the usual low-priced theatrical lodgings were already occupied. So he decided to treat himself and stay at a first-class private hotel, though it was really more than he could afford.

The room was a well furnished and comfortable one. For the first three nights he was there, Browne found himself afflicted by nightmares, which disrupted his sleep. At first he thought that he was eating something that didn't agree with him. He tried changing his diet, but it didn't seem to work. This was very disturbing to Browne, who felt that as an actor he needed more sleep than most people in order to keep up his energy for a performance.

On the fourth night he fell asleep quickly but after a short time was awakened by a loud crash. "Wondering what on earth the noise could have been, and feeling very thirsty, I got out of bed to get a drink of lime juice."

The glass of lime juice was on the mantelpiece, but stumbling around in the dark, Browne was unable to find it. He also couldn't find a box of matches so he could light a candle.

Finally, after breaking an ashtray and a soap dish, he decided to give up and go back to bed. Then he couldn't find the bed! It was a small room, and at first Brown laughed. "Fancy not being able to find one's way back to bed in a room of this size." However, after groping his way around the room a couple of times, the actor became alarmed. "Could I be ill? Was I going mad?"

Browne determined to walk straight across the room. He ran into something that hit him in the face. When he put up his hand to find out what it was, he felt a thick rope that ended in a noose.

The noose moved like a snake and dropped over his head. Hard as he tried, Browne was unable to get it off. "Cold, clammy hands tore my feet from the floor; I was hoisted bodily up, and then let drop. A frightful pain shot through me . . ."

Browne struggled for breath until he finally became unconscious. When he recovered consciousness, the actor found himself standing on the cold floor, shivering, but otherwise unhurt. He now found it easy to get back to his bed and fell asleep almost immediately. When he woke up, he tried to persuade himself that it all had been another nightmare.

As you might imagine, he did not relish going to bed the next evening. He determined to keep a candle burning all night. Much to his surprise, he fell asleep quickly. And when he awoke, the room was pitch dark. The first thing he noticed was the smell—the strong, pungent odor of drugs and chemicals. It reminded him of a chemist's shop or his old school laboratory.

Then he felt something cold and flabby in the bed beside him. "In an agony of fear I reeled away from it, and, the bed being narrow, I slipped over the edge and bumped onto the floor."

Groping around, he found a candle and was able to light it. And it was then he saw that his bed was occupied by a figure—and when he looked closely he saw that the face was that of his brother Ralph. Ralph lived in New York and was the only member of Browne's family who was making any real money at that time.

He called out, "Ralph," and quickly wished he hadn't.

"The moment I did so, there was a ghastly change: His eyelids opened, and his eyes protruded to such a degree that they almost rolled out; his mouth flew open, his tongue swelled . . ." It was the face of a man who had choked to death.

Then the figure spoke. The voice was raspy and hollow, but recognizably Ralph's. "I have been dead a month; not cancer, but Dolly. Poison. Good-bye. I shall rest now."

Suddenly there was a rush of cold air through the room and the horrible apparition vanished.

In the morning came a letter from Browne's mother, saying that she had just heard from Dolly, Ralph's wife, saying that Ralph had died of cancer of the throat. In a postscript she added that Ralph had left her very well provided for.

Browne said that they might have asked to have the body exhumed, but his family was poor, and Ralph's widow was now rich and lived in America. "You know, everything goes in favor of the dollars." So they let the matter drop, assuming that Dolly would never come to visit them. And she never did.

Later Browne discovered that the hotel that he had stayed in had a long-standing reputation for being haunted. People who slept in one of the rooms, presumably the room he had been in, often complained of hearing strange noises and having terrible dreams.

"How can one explain it all?" he asked O'Donnell.

"One can't," O'Donnell responded.

CHAPTER ELEVEN

MEETING ON THE ROAD

WHEN GABRIEL FISHER left the White Bull tavern, it was already quite dark. Perhaps he had a bit more to drink than usual. But he had his wits about him, and he knew the walk home would sober him up nicely. On his journey home, he was accompanied by his dog Trotty, which, true to its name, trotted alongside him.

At that time of night, the road was empty and extremely quiet. Man and dog had reached about the halfway point in the journey home when Fisher heard a high-pitched scream. He was startled, even frightened. Trotty began to whine.

Fisher peered into the gloom to see if he could locate the source of the scream. In the distance he could see a figure, walking slowly. As he got closer he could just make out it was a woman wearing a cloak and a large bonnet. It must have been the woman who screamed. But why? And what was she doing walking alone on a deserted road at this time of night?

As Fisher pondered these questions, he drew closer to the figure. The closer they got, the more unhappy Trotty became, until he finally just turned tail and ran away. Fisher's shouts could not bring him back.

When Fisher drew up alongside the woman, he saw that she was carrying a large cloth-covered market basket on her arm. Her head was bowed and completely concealed by the bonnet.

Fisher asked the woman if she was all right and if it was she who had screamed. Her answers were muffled. He could not make them out, for they seemed to come from far away. But the tone of the voice was pleasant and almost hypnotically attractive.

They walked side by side for a short time, and then Gabriel Fisher, remembering his manners, asked the woman if he might carry the basket for her. She handed him the basket.

As he hooked his arm into the handle, came the reply, "You're much too kind." It was followed by a laugh, a light bubbling laugh, but one that contained an unpleasant hint of mockery. What was most puzzling, however, was that the voice and laugh did not seem to come from the woman.

He turned to look at her more closely, but she was looking away, apparently examining something on the side of the road. And again came that laugh. More mockingly this time, and definitely not from the woman. The laugh was coming from the basket he carried on his arm!

Horrified, Fisher flung the basket away. It hit the ground, bounced, and something rolled out—a woman's head.

Fisher whirled about to face his companion. She was standing directly beside him now, and turned toward him. Her bonnet had been thrown back onto her shoulders, revealing, most horribly, that she had no head. The figure's shoulders shook, as if she were laughing. But the sound of the laughter issued from the mouth of the head on the ground.

After a second or two in which he was too paralyzed with fear to do anything, Fisher took off running down the road, faster than he had ever run before. He looked back just long enough to see the figure of the woman, now holding the head in her hand, fling the dreadful object directly at him.

It was a mighty toss, for the head struck the earth near him, bounced up of its own accord, and flew past him. Its eyes were glittering, and its teeth were snapping dangerously.

The head then rolled near his feet, still snapping like an angry dog. Fisher very nearly fell over it. He now became aware that the body was also running up the road. And it was gaining on him.

Then the terrified man saw a small stream. Somewhere in the back of his mind he remembered a bit of folklore that he had heard as a child. He had been told that a ghost could not cross moving water. He immediately splashed through the stream and kept on running until he reached the top of a hill. Too exhausted to take another step, Gabriel Fisher stopped and looked back. There, on the other side of the stream, stood the headless woman. At its feet rolled the head, its eyes blazing, screaming with fury at having been deprived of its victim.

The horrible sight gave Fisher new strength, and he started running again. This time he ran all the way home. There he was greeted by the still-trembling Trotty and by his wife, who was not very sympathetic when he told his story. She replied that it appeared to take a headless woman to get him to learn the value of coming home early.

When he repeated the tale to his neighbors, they tended to laugh and hint that he was pulling their leg, or perhaps that he had been drunk at the time. But in fact, no one who heard the story was ever known to venture along that particular stretch of road at night anymore. And many would not go down it even in the daytime.

CHAPTER TWELVE

THE BANDAGED HORROR

IN JULY 1884 three survivors from the wreck of the British yacht *Pierrot* were found floating in a battered dinghy in the Atlantic by the yacht *Gellert*. The men had been adrift for almost a month, and were near death from starvation and exposure.

At first the three men, Captain Edward Rutt, mate Josh Dudley, and seaman Will Hoon, said that they were the only ones to have escaped the sinking. But hidden under a tarpaulin was the body of another member of the crew, eighteen-year-old seaman Dick Tomlin. More appalling still was evidence that the young man's body had been partially eaten!

Cannibalism, while horrifying, was not unknown among starving shipwrecked survivors. The question for the crew of the *Gellert* was, how did Tomlin die? At first the three survivors said that they decided to eat their young shipmate only after he had died of natural causes. But a close examination of the body determined that he had died not from natural causes but from a knife wound in the neck.

As soon as that discovery was made, the whole story came out. The four survivors had been adrift for twenty-five days. Death from starvation seemed inevitable when Captain Rutt made a desperate suggestion. Lots should be drawn to determine which of the four would be killed and eaten.

Dudley and Hoon agreed to the suggestion. Tomlin, however, protested that he would rather die than become a cannibal. That sealed his fate. At the first opportunity Rutt stabbed the boy. They were rescued by the *Gellert* four days after the killing.

Once they returned to England, Rutt, Dudley, and Hoon were tried for murder and condemned to death. But the Home Secretary decided that the circumstances under which the murder had been committed were so extreme that he commuted the death sentence to a mere six months' imprisonment. As it turned out, he did not do the three men a favor.

When the men were freed from jail, they found themselves shunned by almost everyone. Their names were well known among sailors, and they could not find work on any ship in England. Josh Dudley got a job as a drayman, handling large wagons used to haul freight. Two weeks after he started work, his horses saw something that frightened them in the middle of a foggy London street. They bolted and tossed Dudley to the cobblestone streets, where he struck his head and received a fatal wound.

Witnesses said that just before the accident, they had seen a strange figure standing in the street. It looked, they said, like a man swathed from head to foot in bloodstained bandages like a mummy. But with the fog they could not be sure. Immediately after the accident, the figure vanished.

Captain Rutt heard of his former mate's death and became badly frightened. He sought out the third survivor, Will Hoon. But the old seaman had been virtually destroyed by his experiences. He had become a hopeless drunk and was living in poverty and squalor in one of London's worst slums.

Rutt tried to convince Hoon that they were being pursued by a relative of Dick Tomlin, bent on vengeance. This, not the young man's ghost, was the danger to them, he said. Hoon was almost beyond caring.

A short time later he was taken off to the charity hospital, where he died in a violent alcoholic fit. Witnesses at the hospital said that another patient, covered in bandages, had been holding the wildly screaming and thrashing Hoon down, apparently to keep him from injuring himself. No one was sure who the bandaged patient was.

Rutt was now absolutely terrified. Relative or ghost—someone was out to get him, of that he was sure. He went to the police for protection, but they just laughed at his story. Still, in view of the former captain's obvious fear, they offered to lock him up. It was an offer Rutt gratefully accepted.

He was put into a cell in a section of the prison used for the violent mentally ill. It was a part of the prison where screams in the night were common. But there was something different about the screams that began coming from Rutt's cell at about three in the morning. The warders immediately unlocked the door. They were too late. The former captain lay in the corner, his knees drawn up to his chest, his hands crossed. He was dead.

Most shocking of all, they found shreds of bloodstained linen clutched in his dead hand.

CHAPTER THIRTEEN

THE DEATH CAR RETURNS

ONE OF THE MOST WIDELY told ghostly tales in America is the one that folklorists call "The Death Car." The core of the story is that there is a car haunted by the ghost of the gangster or someone who had once owned the car and was killed in it. Here are a couple of lesser-known versions of this popular tale.

During the Prohibition era there was a Chicago gang leader called "Red" Halloran. He had a lot of money, but he also had a lot of enemies on both sides of the law. He had a car custom built for himself. It was a huge, powerful, sixteen-cylinder car, faster than anything else on the road, and it was completely bulletproof—well, almost completely. One day when Red was driving all by himself just outside of Chicago, he ran into a police ambush. The armor on his car didn't protect him, and he was shot to death.

Somehow the gangster's magnificent car wound up with an auto dealer in New York State. Then it was purchased by a man who lived in California and collected fancy cars. Normally someone would be hired to drive the car cross-country. But the history of this car was well known. And it had a bad reputation. None of the men who usually did cross-country driving wanted to spend several days in this particular car.

Finally the dealer found a newspaper reporter who had just lost his job and wanted badly to go to California to find a new one. He was given one hundred dollars, plus expenses, to make the trip. But the mechanics at the garage where he picked up the car told him he would never get it past Chicago. The reporter paid no attention to such superstitious fears.

In order to save the money that he otherwise would have spent on motel rooms, the reporter decided to sleep in the car during the trip. It was certainly big enough.

The first part of the trip was uneventful. The car behaved exactly as an expensive car should. Somewhere in Illinois the reporter began to get sleepy again. He pulled over onto a side road, locked the doors, and took a nap. He was rudely awakened by a sudden motion of the car. It was being driven at top speed by a muscular redheaded man whom he had never seen before and who would not even acknowledge his presence. The redhead just kept whistling "Yankee Doodle" and driving at top speed.

After a few miles, during which the reporter was growing increasingly panicky, he saw that there were police cars with flashing lights on the roadside ahead. Instead of slowing, the car actually speeded up and whizzed past the police, completely ignoring their signals to stop. That's when the police started shooting.

The reporter was shocked into action. He reached over to the driver's side. With one hand he grabbed the wheel. With the other he turned off the ignition. The car coughed, slowed, and stopped. And the reporter realized that he was all alone inside. The redheaded man had disappeared.

When the reporter tried to explain to the police what had taken place, he realized just how thin the story sounded. He fully expected to be arrested. But a couple of the officers had actually seen two figures in the car. And when they heard the reporter's description of the mysterious driver, they all knew why he had disappeared. They had set up their roadblock in the same spot where police, a few years before, had shot the notorious Red Halloran while trying to run a similar roadblock. The police told the reporter he was free to go but that he should forget what had happened because no one was going to believe him anyway.

Then they went back to waiting for the stolen car they had been looking for in the first place.

In 1960 seventeen-year-old Janet Hernandez bought her first car—a secondhand 1952 Ford Victoria. It was a great bargain at only $275.

While polishing her car—something the owner of his or her first car does often—she noticed that three round holes in the passenger-side door had been patched. Someone had done a good job of patching, because the holes weren't visible at a casual glance. But up close they were obvious.

Janet thought that the holes looked like bullet holes. And she imagined that someone riding in the car had been shot—and that was why the car had been so cheap. But the car ran fine and it looked great, so she didn't worry about its history. At least she didn't worry until things started happening.

"While we were riding around the block on one of our first outings in the car, the vehicle's passenger door flew open. We didn't think much of it and took the car to the garage for repair. The mechanic couldn't find anything wrong . . ."

But later the door kept flying open. "I told Dad. He checked the door catch over again but still could find nothing wrong."

Yet no one thought too much about this peculiarity until the door began flying open when the car was going 40 m.p.h. or more. That was beginning to get dangerous. And it seemed to happen whenever the car was driven past a cemetery, though it didn't seem to make any difference which cemetery.

Now Janet realized that something strange was going on. She took the car in for an oil change. While the car was up on the lift, the mechanic noticed that the exhaust system was being held on by wires. Something had very definitely happened to the car. "Our bargain was turning into a real mystery!" Janet said. The mechanic replaced the wires with clamps, and Janet took the car out for a spin.

This time the passenger-side door flew open while the car was going 50 m.p.h.

"Have you ever tried to push a door open at that speed?" she said. "Pretty difficult." Janet decided that her car was haunted by someone who had been killed in a shootout. She also decided that she didn't want a haunted car and was going to sell this one at the first opportunity.

In the meantime her father secured the passenger-side door with a strong rope. As Janet was driving past a little church near the center of town, the rope snapped and the door flew open once again. A cemetery was located behind the church.

An hour later she was able to sell the car for $650. She never said anything about the car being haunted, and she was able to make money on the deal. She never heard any more about the 1952 Ford.

"Perhaps the ghost had its last ride."

CHAPTER FOURTEEN

THE BLOODSTONE RING

PEOPLE HAVE ALWAYS been fascinated by stories of brides who disappeared mysteriously on their wedding day. But here is one such account in which the missing bride may actually have come back—well, sort of.

In the 1870s Mrs. Elizabeth Grey was a well-to-do widow who lived with her two young daughters in the fashionable English resort village of Boscombe, near the sea. The girls, Mary and Ellen, were very close to each other—more like twins, some people said, than just sisters.

But they didn't look like twins. Mary, who was two years younger than Ellen, was prettier, livelier, and by far the more popular of the two. There was always a crowd of young men hanging around her, and it seemed that they all wanted to marry her.

Mary relished the attention and the flattery, but she put off all her would-be suitors by telling them that she was too young to be thinking seriously about marriage. And that was the truth.

But there was one, a persistent and rather dour fellow named John Bodneys, who simply could not be put off so easily. He was twenty-three years old, some six years older than Mary. As the son of a successful lawyer who seemed destined for a successful career in the law himself, he was what most would have considered a "good catch." And there was no doubt that he loved Mary—indeed, it might even have been said that he was obsessed by her.

And that was the problem, for Bodneys's constant pressing irritated Mary. One day he insisted that she tell him if she would marry him. When she once again said that she was simply too young to make up her mind, he said, "Mary, you must give me an answer. I'll wait a year if you like—until you're eighteen, old enough to know your own mind."

"Oh, very well," she answered carelessly. "I suppose you may ask me again then. But don't shout so, or look so black, or you'll frighten me and I won't answer you at all."

During the next year Mary did indeed change. She became quieter and more serious. Bodneys took this as a sign that she was growing up and that a more mature Mary would certainly say yes to his proposal.

Bodneys was partly correct. Mary had become more mature, and she had decided on her future husband—but he was not John Bodneys. She had met a young man named Basil Osborne, a newcomer to the area, and had fallen in love with him immediately.

Osborne was to turn twenty-one the week before Mary had her eighteenth birthday, and the couple decided to hold off announcing their engagement until then.

Mary's mother urged her to tell Bodneys of her engagement before it was announced publicly. If everybody else knew first, he might be humiliated. But Mary said no, the engagement was a secret and she did not want to spoil it. Besides, she would be telling him before her eighteenth birthday was over, and at least technically she would have kept her promise. In truth, she didn't really care much one way or the other.

The morning after the couple announced their plans at a large party, Mary sat down and wrote John Bodneys a brief letter explaining her decision. She received no reply.

At one point Mary's sister, Ellen, thought she had spotted Bodneys in the woods near the house, but she could not be sure. The incident was completely forgotten in the preparations for the wedding, which was just weeks away.

After the wedding there was a simple reception held at the home of Mary's mother. As the reception was ending, Mary went upstairs to her room to change out of her wedding dress into traveling clothes, in preparation for her honeymoon trip. Her sister accompanied her to the room. But Mary said that she wanted a few minutes alone to say good-bye to the room in which she had grown up. It held many happy memories, and now she would be leaving it forever.

"I'll call you when I'm ready," said Mary. "I won't be long."

Ellen looked back and saw her sister, still in her bridal

gown, standing by the window. It was the last time anyone ever saw Mary alive.

The wedding party waited downstairs for about half an hour for Mary to come down. When she didn't Ellen went upstairs to fetch her. But the door to the bedroom was locked, and when she called to Mary, there was no answer.

After Ellen told the wedding party downstairs about the locked door, Basil determined to break the door down. With the assistance of some of the other young men, this was swiftly accomplished. The room was empty. Mary's traveling clothes were still laid out neatly on the bed. It looked as if Mary were getting ready to change into them.

The missing bride wasn't on the balcony, but on the flight of small steps that led from the balcony to the garden below, searchers found a white rose that the bride had worn on her dress during the wedding ceremony.

The surrounding countryside was searched. No trace of Mary was found. Checks were made at the railway stations and the ports—surely a young woman wearing a wedding dress would have been noticed by someone. But no one came forward. Advertisements were placed in all the newspapers. There were no believable responses.

Local people were divided as to what they thought had happened. Some were sure that Mary had suffered a "brain storm"—a quaint Victorian term that meant suddenly going crazy—as a result of the stresses of the wedding, and had rushed to the sea, which was not too far off, and drowned herself.

Others, remembering the young woman's many suitors,

suggested that she had a secret lover and had run off with him. If so, he was not John Bodneys, for he remained at home, a silent and unapproachable man. Some months later, he went abroad and was not seen again in the neighborhood.

Years passed, but Mary's tragic disappearance continued to take its toll. Mrs. Grey died just a few years after her daughter vanished. Basil Osborne did not remarry, even after Mary had been missing long enough to be officially declared dead. He lived on in the house that he had once expected to share with his bride. He became something of a recluse, his health suffered, and he too died within a few years.

Only Ellen remained. She stayed at the house where she and her sister had grown up. She became increasingly strange, and the few people who visited her wondered if she were not a little mad. Her only regular companion was one servant, Maggie Williams, who had grown up with the sisters and had been devoted to them.

A little more than eighteen years after the disappearance, there was a great coastal storm. Fishing boats were swamped. Roofs were blown off. And of course, many ancient trees were uprooted. One of them was a huge oak tree that had stood near the top of a cliff. When it fell it brought down a lot of rocks and boulders, and the debris completely blocked the road.

Workmen were sent to clear the road. While they were digging, one of them peered into a cleft between two large rocks. He saw something red and shiny, surrounded by what at first looked like whitish twigs. But when the rocks were moved, he found that what he had seen was a ring with a red stone in it, and what had looked like twigs were the bones of a human hand.

More searching revealed the entire skeleton—a rather dainty one, probably that of a young woman. There were a few scattered bits of cloth clinging to the bones, but not enough to clearly identify any article of clothing. But the red stone ring, which turned out to be garnet, or bloodstone, and a second ring, a wedding band that was worn on the same finger, were enough to provide an identification.

As soon as the remains were brought to the village, one of the older residents, who had attended the wedding reception eighteen years before, said, "It must be poor Mary Osborne."

Ellen was sent for. She arrived at the police station wearing black, as she always had since her sister vanished. She examined the remains and said, "That is the garnet engagement ring she wore on her wedding day. It is my sister."

Shortly before the remains were to be buried, Ellen made a request of the undertaker. She wanted her sister's hand, the one that contained the rings. The undertaker was surprised, but not as shocked as a modern undertaker might be. In Victorian times it was not uncommon to keep relics of the dead— usually something like a lock of hair. The bones of a hand were unusual, but he could see no valid reason for refusing the request, so Ellen was given the skeleton hand.

Ellen kept the skeleton hand with its rings displayed on a black velvet cushion in a glass box. The minister's wife, one of her few visitors, was horrified by the grisly trophy, which she regarded as blasphemous.

She was afraid to talk directly to Ellen, whom she now regarded as completely mad. But she did protest to the servant, Maggie.

"It won't do you no good, ma'am," said Maggie Williams. "She's set on keeping it, and I'm to have it when she's gone."

Certainly, said the minister's wife to the servant, she would not keep the gruesome thing, but would have the hand decently reburied.

"Never, ma'am," replied Maggie. "She says she'll *walk* if I do. And I don't want no haunting."

Ellen died a little more than a year after the discovery of her sister's remains. Hours before Ellen died, Maggie questioned her mistress once again about keeping the hand. "For I can't see what good it'll do, ma'am, to her that's gone."

"One day it will avenge her, Maggie," the dying woman said. "I cannot tell you how, but I know this to be true."

Ellen Grey left most of her money to her faithful servant. Maggie now had enough to buy a small pub that she could run by herself. She had the place completely renovated. Prominently displayed on the bar was the glass case with the skeleton hand. Maggie remained true to her vow. Besides, she was a shrewd businesswoman and figured that the grisly relic, which was now well known in the area, would attract some customers.

She was quite right. Hardly a night went by when a customer did not comment on it. The story of Mary's disappearance was told and retold endlessly to newcomers at the pub.

One evening while a storm was raging outside, one of the

pub's regulars began to reminisce loudly. "It was on a night like this when the great oak came down. Maybe they'd never have found the skeleton but for that."

A tall man, whose face was half hidden by his turned-up collar and pulled-down cap, had been drinking at the far corner of the bar. He was a stranger, not one of the regulars, and he suddenly spoke up: "What skeleton?"

"Why, that skeleton," said Maggie from behind the bar. And she pointed to the skeleton hand in the glass case. "Don't you know the story?"

The stranger didn't say anything. He stared at the glass box. Then he went over to it, and put his hand on top of the box. Some in the bar swore that blood began to flow from his fingers. Everyone saw that he crumpled to the floor.

Two men took him to a bench, took off his cap, and loosened his collar. When the man's face was fully revealed, Maggie realized that it was a familiar one, though she had not seen it in nearly twenty years.

"Mr. Bodneys?" she said.

"Yes, I'm John Bodneys. I never meant to come back here. But I had to. Something drew me like a magnet."

"You killed her—our Miss Mary?"

"Yes, I killed her."

Bodneys then went on to tell the story of what had happened. How he had waited in the woods near the house. How, mad with jealousy, he had climbed into Mary's room when he saw her at the window, and confronted her. How he had struck her unconscious and carried her off when she re-

fused to go with him. And how she had regained consciousness and struggled free on the path near the waterfall. Finally
he described how she stumbled and fell, down between the
rocks. He ran away, not knowing if she were dead or alive
though he later learned of her death. He told the story completely and without hesitation, as if he had repeated it hun-
dreds of times before—and he had, but until then only to
himself.

"I have been in hell these many years. I know they'll hang
me as I deserve."

But he didn't hang. He died, though no one could determine the cause, shortly before he was brought to trial.

Maggie had the hand with its rings buried with the rest of
Mary's remains. As her sister had said, it had done its aveng-
ing work and now could rest.

CHAPTER FIFTEEN

WAITING IN THE SHADOWS

THIS STRANGE ACCOUNT appeared in the British publication *Blackwood's Magazine* in January 1891, and it was said to be a true story.

The account was written by an officer in the British army. The events described happened a long time ago, when the officer "was a very raw young ensign." But he insists "the circumstances in this case were such that they have indelibly fixed themselves in my recollection, as though they had occurred yesterday."

The regiment with which the narrator had been serving was stationed on the island of Malta. The chief actor was a man he will identify only as Ralph D——.

D—— himself had once been an officer in the British army

in India. But he left the service for some vague and unexplained reason. He then joined up with the Austrian cavalry, "as not a few British ex-officers managed at that time to do." But once again he left for unexplained reasons.

D— had drifted to Malta, where he lived comfortably among the large British colony on the island. He was a well-known character, popular with but not really trusted by his countrymen. He seemed to support himself primarily by gambling. D— never was known to lose at cards, and there were ominous whispers that he cheated, though nothing was ever proven. And he made such a charming companion that he never lacked for others to join him in a game.

One of the things that many visitors to Malta find most memorable are the religious processions during Holy Week, the week before Easter. The streets are crowded with men wearing dark robes and hoods, who are part of the processions.

On Holy Thursday, the day before Good Friday, the narrator had gone to the other side of the Grand Harbour to visit a friend and to view the religious processions and listen to the music. He returned to his barracks after dark.

"I should here explain," he wrote, "that Thursdays were guest nights of my regiment at that time, and on this evening the regimental band had as usual been playing in the open space just outside; fronting the officers' dining hall windows. It must have been past eleven o'clock when I reached barracks; and although most of the outsiders who were allowed in to hear the music on such occasions were gone, I noted two or three still waiting about."

One of them particularly caught his attention. He was a very tall man wearing a dark cloak with a hood. The narrator thought he must have been someone who had dressed up for the religious procession or was a monk from a nearby monastery. The ensign wandered up to his room and, after a while, looked out the window. "By this time the loiterers were all gone except the tall cloaked man, who appeared to have never moved or changed his position since I saw him first . . . Who was this man and what on earth could he be waiting for?"

Then he heard some loud voices and laughter coming from a lit-up room in the officers' dining area. It was obvious that some of the men were playing cards well into the night, as they often did.

The cloaked figure appeared to be staring up toward the lighted room. For some reason he could not define, the narrator said, he felt that the cloaked figure might be dangerous and evil. "I had an awakening consciousness that I had better walk straight over and ask the man what he wanted at that time of night."

But he couldn't do it. He suddenly felt numb and unable to move. It was like a nightmare in which you know something dreadful is about to happen but you can't do anything to stop it. He could see that the cloaked figure was waiting and listening for someone or something in the lighted dining hall. But he could not account for his overpowering feeling of dread and impending evil.

The feeling and the paralysis lasted only a few seconds. Then he heard loud voices coming from the lighted room. It sounded as if some sort of argument was going on. One familiar voice was louder than all of the others. It was easy to recognize D—'s hard and distinct accent.

"I seem to hear the words rasping now as I write. 'I tell you, I dealt myself the ace of spades'; then another voice, young N—'s, 'I take my oath you didn't.' "

D— began to swear, and then he called upon "the Prince of Darkness to the ruin of his soul and body, if what he had stated was not the truth."

That was what the cloaked figure had been waiting for. He jumped to the window with the agility of a cat and disappeared through the curtains into the room. In another moment there was a scream, "a harsh, appalling cry as of mingled pain, rage, and terror . . . and to my horror and utter amazement the man in the cloak reappeared at the window with D— gripped in his arms, and half slung over one shoulder, apparently struggling desperately."

The ensign rushed out of his room, but the robed figure and his victim had already disappeared around the corner of the building. There was no one else there who might have seen or been able to stop them. He shouted for the guards, and they came, but a search of the grounds revealed nothing.

When he returned to the dining hall area, the ensign found that it was the scene of great excitement. In the room where the game of cards had taken place, a group of young officers was gathered around the overturned card table. Cards littered the floor. Also on the floor was D—. The regimental surgeon came in after a minute or two, examined D—, and shook his head. The man was dead.

"As for myself, I could hardly believe my senses. The man I had just seen bodily carried off struggling in the arms of an unknown individual, lying here dead—it seemed an absolute hallucination! I was too taken aback to ask a single question . . ."

A few days later he did find out what had happened. D— and a half dozen young officers had dinner, then sat down to play cards. The stakes were high, and D— was winning heavily. During one game when D— was dealing, another player was dealt the ace of spades. Later in the game, D— himself turned over the ace of spades, the card that would have made him a winner. Obviously someone was cheating, and that is what led to the shouting the narrator overheard.

Those who witnessed the argument felt a gust of wind and what seemed to be the tremor of a slight earthquake. But they saw no robed figure. What they did see was D— clutch his chest and fall back in his chair, as if he had had a heart attack or some sort of fit. The official cause of death was listed as heart attack.

The whole thing was hushed up because talk of cheating at cards would have been an embarrassment to the regiment and to D—'s family.

The narrator said that he would have been inclined to dismiss the man in the cloak as "a phantasm of my own brain" had he not talked to another man in the barracks. This fellow had been sick, and on that Thursday night had been lying on a couch in his room, by the open window. He had been listening to the band.

The narrator and his friend were discussing the events of the fatal Thursday night. As soon as the subject of D—'s death was touched upon, the sick officer "broke in with a very troubled face, and in a serious voice asked: 'Did you see the man in the long cloak waiting for him?' "

CHAPTER SIXTEEN

THE LAST TENANT

IN NEW YORK STATE not long ago, there was a major legal controversy over whether someone selling or renting a house had to disclose whether the house was supposedly haunted.

But in Scotland it is illegal to say a house is haunted if that hurts the chances of selling or renting the property. And it doesn't make any difference if the place really *is* haunted.

A family called the Gordons was prevented from giving the address of the house in which they had a most terrifying ghostly experience when the landlord threatened them with a lawsuit for what is called "slander of property."

In a sense the landlord was right. Some people may like the idea of sharing a house with a nice, friendly, well-behaved ghost. This one was anything but. No one who ever heard the

Gordons' story would ever want to rent any place occupied by the ghost they encountered.

The house didn't look haunted. It wasn't particularly ancient either, at least in terms of the city of Edinburgh, in which it was located. The house was some eighty years old when the Gordons moved in. It was quite a large place and had been broken up into flats and shops and offices. What the Scots call the ground floor and first floor, which Americans would call the first and second floors, had been converted into small shops and office space. The Gordons rented a large flat on the second floor. The top floor was unoccupied and apparently used just for storage.

Within a week of the family's moving in, Mrs. Gordon knew that something was wrong. At night she heard the footsteps of someone rushing up the stairs to the top floor. The footsteps made so much noise that it was keeping her awake. She complained about the noise to the landlord, but he assured her that he knew nothing about it.

"I can't imagine who is making the noise," he said blandly. "It may be someone next door, sounds are so often deceptive, particularly at night. But I assure you the rooms above you are unoccupied."

Mrs. Gordon wasn't entirely convinced. The next night she lay awake, listening for the sounds. At first nothing happened. She was, however, oppressed by a nearly overpowering sense of evil, as though something sinister and hostile had entered the room. She was too terrified even to turn on the light.

Then she heard the "thing"—she could find no better

words to describe it—go out to the landing and rush up the stairs. For what must have been half an hour, she heard the sound of someone in boots running around the empty rooms above.

The next morning at breakfast, Mrs. Gordon asked her daughters if they had heard any noises in the night. "No, nothing. Not even a mouse," they laughingly replied.

Mrs. Gordon felt rather foolish. She mentally wrote the whole incident off as a bad dream. And for the next several weeks, nothing unusual happened. Then Mrs. Gordon went away on a trip, and her eldest daughter, Diana, a young woman with a reputation for a realistic and no-nonsense approach to life, took over her mother's bedroom. One evening Diana was in the bedroom just before dinner. Suddenly the bedroom door swung open and something, she could not tell what, rushed past her and onto the landing. With a great clatter of what sounded like heavy boots, the thing quickly went upstairs to the empty rooms.

At first Diana was more curious than frightened. She ran up the stairs and heard a terrific racket in the room above her mother's.

Unafraid, she went to the door and threw it open. There was something—she could see only a vague and filmy outline—standing in front of a large clock, which apparently it was winding.

Now she was afraid. What was the thing? What if it should turn around and see her? She was all alone in the fading light and in a big spooky room full of old furniture. She was completely paralyzed with fear for a moment. The thing seemed to be too busy with the clock to take any notice of her. Then it stopped winding and appeared to be at the point of turning around. At that moment a familiar voice calling her to dinner floated up from the floor below. That broke the spell. Diana turned and ran downstairs, not noticing what reaction the shape at the clock had to the sudden activity.

When Diana got her breath back, she described to her sister what had happened. Neither one suggested that they go upstairs to investigate any further. Diana moved back into the room with her sister, though they got little sleep that night.

Nothing else happened until Mrs. Gordon returned. The evening after she got back, as she was preparing to go to bed, the door to her bedroom swung open. Standing there was the figure of a man. He was short, with huge shoulders and long arms. He was wearing a pea jacket (a kind of coat commonly worn by seamen), baggy trousers, and heavy boots. His large head was covered with a tangled mass of yellowish hair. But of his face Mrs. Gordon could see almost nothing, for he was standing in the shadows. He was carrying what appeared to be a small bundle of red and white rags in one hand.

While Mrs. Gordon was staring at this strange and terrifying figure, it suddenly swung around, rushed to the landing, and, in a series of jumps, disappeared up the staircase.

That was it! Unlike the characters in so many horror films who stay in the haunted house after repeated warnings and encounters with the ghost, Mrs. Gordon did not want to chance another encounter. She and her daughters packed up and moved out that very next morning. As the report spread that the house was haunted, Mrs. Gordon got a series of indignant and threatening letters from her former landlord. That is why she would never give the address of the house in which she had lived.

Mrs. Gordon also got letters about the early history of the house and possible reasons for the haunting. Only one of these letters sounded plausible. It said that some years before, the rooms she had rented had been occupied by a retired captain in the Merchant Service.

He was a strange man, the letter said, who continued to wear nautical clothes despite the fact that he had not been on a ship in years. He was also a very heavy drinker. The drink was rapidly destroying his mind.

At the time, the rooms above the captain's were rented to a couple who had a small infant. The baby's crying annoyed the captain. He warned the baby's mother that if she did not keep her child quiet, he would not be answerable for the consequences. But the warnings appeared to have no effect. One day, in a drunken rage, he ran upstairs when the mother was temporarily away, and killed the infant with a knife he found on the kitchen table. He then stuffed the body into a large clock that stood in a corner of the room.

Of course, the crime was discovered almost immediately and the captain was found in his own rooms, drunk and unconscious. He was arrested on a charge of murder, but was found to be insane and was committed to a lunatic asylum.

Within a few years he killed himself.

Mrs. Gordon was never able to confirm the contents of the letter, and she didn't try. This seemed a possible explanation for the phenomenon. But she did not know if it were true. All she knew was what she had seen. And as far as she and her daughters were concerned, that was more than enough.

CHAPTER SEVENTEEN

SOMETHING IN
THE ROOM

AND FINALLY there is the story told by Colonel Mervyn O'Gorman, who was a pioneer in popularizing the automobile in Britain and a well-known storyteller. He always swore that this story was absolutely true. O'Gorman was an enthusiast about all forms of transportation, and when he was a young man he took up cycling, which was just becoming popular.

One day he cycled from his home to a place called Shipton Manor in Oxfordshire, where he had been invited to spend the weekend at a friend's country estate. It was a long and difficult ride, and he was completely fatigued when he finally arrived. O'Gorman got through dinner, but just barely, and he was so tired that he had to go to bed immediately afterward. His room was a large one but only dimly lit by candles. He was asleep almost the moment his head hit the pillow.

Later that night he awoke. He had heard nothing. He had seen nothing. But he *knew* that there was something in the room with him. He lay there in the darkness, listening.

And then suddenly there was a sound. O'Gorman described it as "a long-drawn shuddering sigh. It ended on a sob, the sob of a tired and weary person." And it originated about a foot away from his head.

The sound terrified him. He couldn't move. Then after about five minutes of straining every nerve to catch another noise, he felt the bed move underneath him. Something heaved the bed upward and then let it down. Once again came that sighing sound. Then nothing.

Despite his terror, O'Gorman was so fatigued that he fell asleep again after about twenty minutes. Then he was awakened again. The room was completely dark, but he knew *it* was still there. And it was moving. He could hear a slow dragging sound. After that came the clink of what must be a chain! The image of a fettered ghost dragging its chains through all eternity came immediately to mind.

Then the most terrifying manifestation of all occurred. The thing in the room reached for the door, which was just about ten feet from O'Gorman's bed. It hit the door with a soft thud, like a pillow that had been thrown against the door. Though the room was almost completely dark, O'Gorman could dimly make out a large formless shape reared up against the door.

Then the shape disappeared. Once again came that sobbing, shuddering sigh.

O'Gorman was now sure that he was alone in a room with the tormented spirit of the victim or perpetrator of some ancient crime. He just lay there in the dark, too frightened to reach for a match or a candle. If there was a light, what terrible thing might be illuminated?

Once again all was quiet. Somehow O'Gorman drifted off to sleep.

At the sound of a footstep, he awoke in terror. But it was light now. A servant had entered the room and was opening the blinds and wishing him good morning. The man turned toward the foot of the bed. Suddenly his jaw dropped. He stared at the floor in disbelief.

"Good heavens, sir," he gasped, "you don't mean to say that our dog has been in here all night, sleeping under the bed. And with his chain on too! Here . . . come out of it, Bruce . . . time you were fed."

DATE			
MAY 31 2006			
SEP 08 2008			